The Best Christmas Ever

ISBN 978-1-09808-555-1 (hardcover)
ISBN 978-1-09808-554-4 (digital)

Christian Faith Publishing
832 Park Avenue
Meadville, PA 16335
www.christianfaithpublishing.com

Printed in the United States of America

The Best Christmas Ever

Matt Nichols

Hannah Bear pulled her scarf tighter around her neck as the cold wind blew and the smell of fresh baked honey cakes from the Three Bears Bakery tickled her nose.

Oh, what a day! This is going to be the best Christmas ever! she said to herself as she headed to Beartown Elementary School.

Just that morning she had flipped the calendar in Mama Bear's kitchen to December.

"This is December! Christmas is almost here!" She was so happy she skipped to school and sang "We Wish You a Merry Christmas" all the way there.

When she arrived at her classroom, the bear children were already hanging their coats and hats and getting ready to start the day. To her delight, her teacher Miss Momirov had put up a beautiful tree, and the bulletin boards were already covered with the winter snowflakes they had made in art class the week before. Miss Momirov was so nice and was always happy to see her students. Hannah Bear rushed to her desk, threw her backpack down, and then ran to Miss Momirov and exclaimed, "Miss Momirov, Miss Momirov, it's going to be wonderful! Christmas is almost here!"

"Well, you're excited today, Hannah Bear!" said Miss Momirov. "Yes, it is almost here, and we need to decorate this tree!"

The bear children opened their art boxes and gathered their supplies. Hannah and her classmates colored, pasted, cut, and stapled and made the most beautiful Christmas ornaments and paper chains the second-grade class at Beartown Elementary School had ever seen. At this point, Hannah Bear could hardly control her happiness. It was all she could do to sit still for the rest of her classes until recess and lunch. She wiggled and fidgeted. She daydreamed about Christmas cookies. She was distracted by the sparkly Christmas lights and watched in amazement out the window as beautiful white snow began to fall.

At recess, Hannah and her friends burned some energy with a game of bear ball.

Huffing and puffing, they finished the game and sat down together on a bench.

"Aren't you all just so excited for Christmas?" Hannah Bear said with a smile so big it could be seen a mile away.

Paisley Bear shrugged. Sarah Bear rolled her eyes. Isaiah Bear looked down and slowly dribbled the ball. She realized that her friends weren't as excited as she was.

"Aren't you guys looking forward to Christmas?" she asked.

Isaiah Bear pushed up his glasses and was the first to speak. He was tall and was one of the smartest bears in the class.

"Well, I'm worried," he said. "I wrote Santa Bear a letter asking for a brand-new ultra, mega, spectacular video gaming system 10,000 deluxe with extra controllers and games. But my Mommy Bear told me she didn't think Santa Bear would be able to bring it this year."

"Oh my," Sarah Bear exclaimed. "There is nothing worse than not getting what you want from Santa Bear. Why does your Mommy Bear think that?"

"She didn't say why," replied Isaiah Bear. "But she was really sad when she told me."

"Oh, how sad," replied the bear friends.

"But if you think that's bad," said Sarah Bear. "Let me tell you why I'm not happy about Christmas this year."

Sarah Bear wore a bright-pink sparkly bow over her left ear and fuzzy pink mittens. Hannah Bear was very surprised.

How could anyone be sad about Christmas? she thought to herself.

Sarah Bear went on to say, "We have to go to my cousin's house for Christmas. And my cousins are just no fun at all. They live far out in the country, and there is absolutely nothing to do. No TV to watch. No stores nearby to shop. And worst of all, my cousins want to play outside all day. They play bear ball, tag, and hide-and-go-seek all day long. And they expect me to play with them the whole time. It's terrible!"

Just as Hannah Bear was about to reply, Paisley Bear chimed in. Paisley Bear had traveled to lots of faraway places and always had the newest toys.

"Oh yeah, well, that's nothing," Paisley Bear said. "We have to go on vacation this year for Christmas. We're going to some place where it's hot and there is an ocean and beach there. I hate getting sand in my fur and stuck in my paws. I am dreading going. I won't know anyone. And my Mommy Bear said I had been a very good bear this year. And I am going to get everything on my Christmas list. I'm getting the newest glamour bear dollhouse extravaganza, a TV for my room, and a new cell phone. And then my Mommy and Daddy Bear are taking me away for an entire week, and I won't be able to play with any of them. It's going to be the worst Christmas ever!"

Paisley Bear frowned and threw her hands up in the air.

Hannah Bear responded, "Well, I just know that…"

Pheeeeeeeeeeeeeee!

And before she could finish her sentence the whistle blew. Miss Momirov called the bears to lunch. The bears ran to form a line and hurriedly went inside to warm up and eat. Hannah Bear was really hungry, and crossed her fingers in hopes that there would be no peas today at the cafeteria. Hannah Bear *hated* peas.

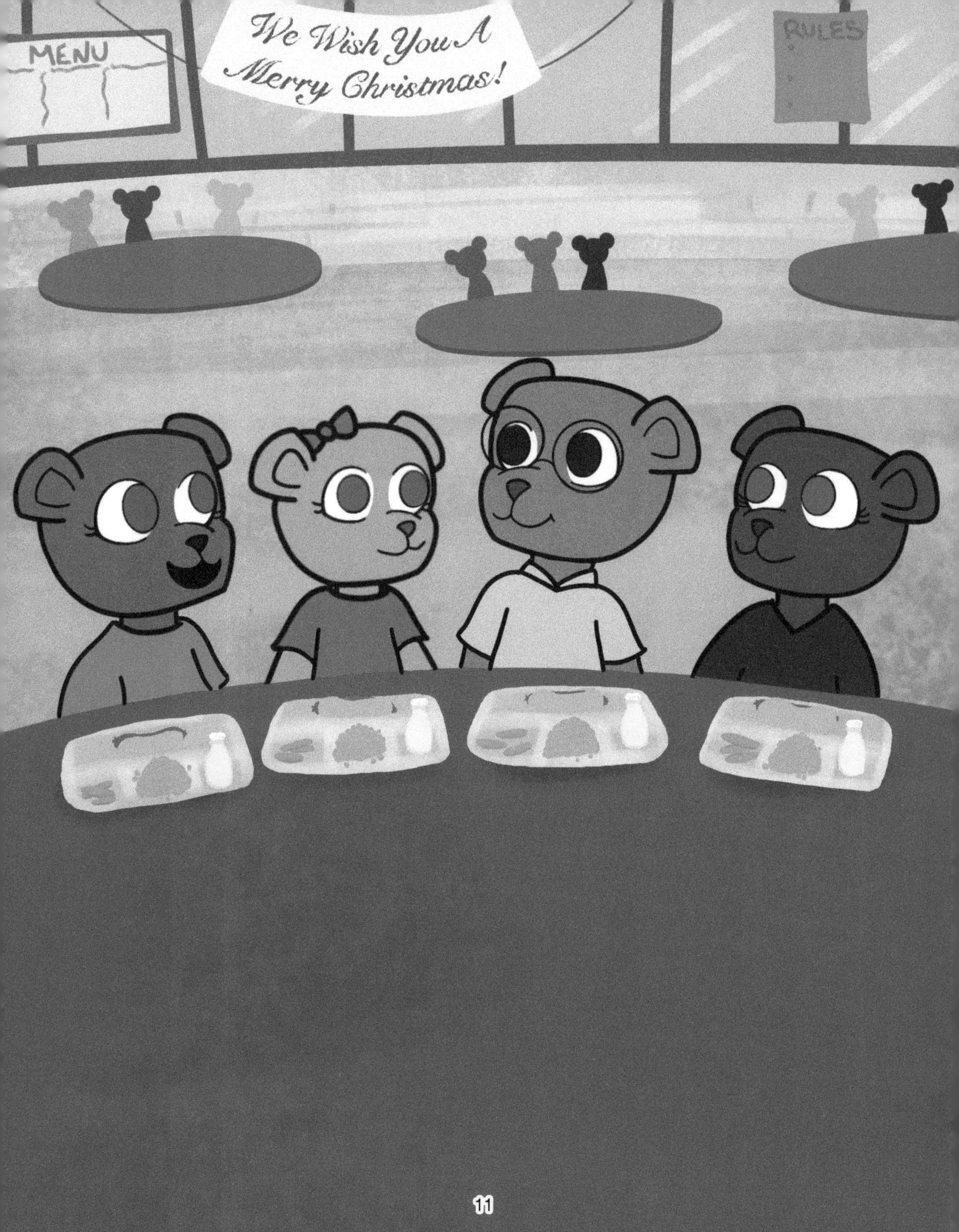
MENU
We Wish You A Merry Christmas!
RULES

As the bear friends sat down, they were all very disgusted with the worst-looking peas the cafeteria at Beartown Elementary School had ever made.

"Gross," said Paisley Bear.

"Nasty," said Isaiah Bear.

Sarah Bear grimaced. "Blech!" she belted out.

But Hannah Bear, who normally hated peas, was not going to allow these gross green circles to ruin her day.

She said, "It's December, and Christmas is almost here! Surely these peas can't be so bad!"

Her friends looked at her like she was crazy!

Her three friends said in unison, "What's so special about Christmas, Hannah Bear?"

"I just love Christmas! It's my favorite day of the year! And it's going to be the best Christmas ever!" replied Hannah.

Just then Hannah Bear was called by Miss Momirov to come help her in the classroom. As she left, Isaiah, Sarah, and Paisley Bear were trying to figure out just how awesome Hannah Bear's Christmas was going to be.

Sarah Bear said, "I'll bet Hannah gets to stay home and watch movies the entire Christmas break! She won't have to play with any cousins or go outside. I'll bet she can do whatever she wants."

Then Paisley Bear said, "Yeah. I'll bet she's getting all the best presents every bear wants, and can stay home and play with them. She's probably getting a cell phone and a laptop and the glamour bear pool to go with her glamour bear dollhouse extravaganza!"

"Wow," said Isaiah Bear. "She probably lives in a really big house with a really big TV with lots of video games."

As the friends talked, they decided that for Hannah, it would definitely be her best Christmas ever!

As the days went by and it got colder and colder in Beartown, the bear friends knew Christmas was almost here. Hannah Bear continued to be excited about Christmas—so much so that her friends began to envy her.

One particular recess when Hannah was playing bear ball, Paisley said to her friends, "I just wish my Christmas was going to be as nice as Hannah's! I am dreading this trip to the beach."

And Isaiah agreed, "Yes, I wish our house was as nice as Hannah's."

And then Sarah Bear had an idea!

She exclaimed, "I know! Tomorrow is Christmas Eve! Why don't we go over to Hannah's house and share Christmas with her! That way, we can all have the best Christmas ever!"

"Excellent idea!" cried Isaiah.

"Yes!" said Paisley. "Let's make a surprise visit to her house tomorrow. That way, we can have as nice a Christmas as Hannah!"

So the next day, the friends met on Center Street right in front of the post office. They began their walk to Hannah Bear's house in great anticipation. Their minds were filled with thoughts of a beautifully decorated mansion with Christmas lights inside and out, video game systems, laptop computers, dollhouse extravaganzas, and a feast topped off with bear pudding!

The streets were lined with houses all decorated for Christmas. Some houses had pretty lighted wreaths on the doors; some had sparkly lights on the porches and trees and candy canes in the yards. There were Santa Bear blowup yard ornaments and reindeer and giant silver bells. But as they got closer to Hannah's house, the houses got smaller and smaller, and the decorations weren't as pretty. Finally, they reached the road that Hannah lived on Rolling Road. As they looked at the house, they thought they might be lost. But they double-checked the cell phone GPS they borrowed from Paisley's Mommy Bear, and they were indeed on the right street. They came to 747 Rolling Road—that was Hannah's house! They had arrived. But their visions of a mansion were quickly diminished.

The house was very small and old. A small plain Christmas wreath hung on the door.

"Surely it must just be wonderful on the inside," Paisley Bear said.

Isaiah Bear knocked. A very tall and scary bear answered the door, "Yes, may I help you?" he asked.

Surprised and nervous, Sarah Bear answered, "We…we…we're here to see Hannah."

Isaiah Bear and Paisley Bear tried to hide behind Sarah Bear. The big bear smiled.

"Why of course, please come in, would you like some hot chocolate?" he asked. "Mama Bear," he called, "we have visitors, pour three mugs of hot chocolate."

The three friends looked at each other and started to relax. Hot chocolate can make anyone feel better.

When the three friends entered the house, several smaller bears ran noisily by. The house was old and plain. The furniture was old and plain. It didn't look anything like they had imagined.

"Is this Hannah Bear's house?" Isaiah said.

"Yes, it is," said the big, tall bear.

"Are you sure?" Sarah Bear piped up, "This is Hannah Bear that goes to Beartown Elementary in the second grade?"

Just then, the friends heard a familiar voice singing "Jingle Bell Bears," and from around the corner appeared the happiest and spunkiest bear in the neighborhood!

"Hi, everyone! What a surprise!" exclaimed Hannah Bear.

Hannah Bear welcomed her friends into her home. Mama Bear appeared with mugs of delicious hot chocolate topped with fluffy peaks of whipped cream. The little bears that were running through earlier were peeking around the corner and giggling. Hannah Bear introduced her brother, sister, and cousins to her friends. Isaiah, Sarah, and Paisley Bear sipped their hot chocolate in awkward silence as they looked around the room. There was no extravagant Christmas tree just a tiny scraggly tree that was leaning to one side. It didn't have beautiful shiny glass ornaments just a handful of homemade paper ornaments. There wasn't a mountain of beautifully wrapped presents under the tree just a few presents wrapped in old newspaper. And there was no big-screen TV. No extravagant dollhouses, and definitely no video game systems.

Finally, when Isaiah Bear couldn't take it anymore, he spoke up and said, "Hannah, I thought you were excited about Christmas. But you are not having a very nice Christmas."

Hannah Bear was bewildered. "What do you mean?" she asked.

"Well, you don't have a big tree, a big house, or lots of presents," said Isaiah.

"And you don't have a big dollhouse," said Paisley.

"And worst of all," said Sarah, "you have a brother and sister and cousins. You have to share your toys, and you can't do what you want all the time."

Although Hannah was surprised at her friends, she took a deep breath and began to explain, "Well, those aren't the things that make Christmas special. Let me show you what makes Christmas special!"

And she led them through the tiny kitchen to the backyard.

The backyard had an old swing set, a huge tree with a tire swing, and a couple of old bear bikes lying on their sides. It looked like a normal backyard for a family with growing bears. But in the middle of the yard was a group of light-up people and animals. There were sheep, camels, cows, and goats. And there were three people dressed up like shepherds, and three other people dressed up like kings. And all the people and animals were lined up facing two people and a baby.

"I've seen that before," said Isaiah, acting not impressed.

"Me too," said Sarah as she flipped her bear hair.

"What is it?" asked Paisley with curiosity.

"That's Baby Jesus and Joseph and Mary and the wise men and the shepherds who came to worship Him!" said Hannah Bear, "Christmas is not about presents or trees! Christmas is about Jesus! I don't need a dollhouse or TV to celebrate Christmas. I have so much joy because Jesus lives in my heart!"

And she explained to her friends that Christmas is a day to celebrate when Jesus was born.

Then Hannah took her friends back inside to her small kitchen. The family was getting ready to eat their Christmas eve dinner. The trio of visiting bears noticed the table was worn. The plates were chipped. But the food smelled delicious. And then they saw a little girl bear in a wheelchair.

"That's Kaitlyn, my little sister," said Hannah with a big smile on her face. "Kaitlyn has a disease. She almost didn't make it this year. We thought we would have to have Christmas without her. And last month, she was able to come home from the hospital. We didn't think she would be home for Christmas. This is the best Christmas ever!"

The big, tall bear had a tear in his big scary bear eye as he listened to Hannah. He wasn't so scary anymore.

He said, "Hannah Bear is right, we almost lost our precious Kaitlyn. We're so thankful she's here, and we're glad you're here too! Would you like to have dinner with us tonight, and celebrate our special Christmas with us?"

The three friends agreed and called their mommy Bears to ask permission. Everyone began to gather for the feast. Hannah's cousins came. And her grandparents. And her aunts and uncles. It was the largest family of bears Isaiah, Sarah, and Paisley had ever seen. And they were all so happy. Even without a big tree and big TV and lots of presents!

And right before the meal started, the front door of the house swung open. A tall, handsome bear wearing an army uniform stepped inside. Hannah and Kaitlyn screamed with joy. It was their big brother bear—Zachary Bear! Zachary

Bear had been gone for over a year as part of the bear army. And now he was home, safe and sound! Hannah's mommy and daddy Bear cried. Kaitlyn Bear turned her wheelchair from side to side to act like she was jumping up and down. And Hannah Bear ran and jumped as high as she could into the strong arms of Zachary her big brother!

Daddy Bear waited until everyone settled down and took time to thank the Lord for their meal, their family being all together, Hannah's friends, and for Jesus being born into the earth. Then they ate an enormous feast of ham and sweet potatoes and noodles and green beans. They had dinner rolls and stuffing and pies.

After dinner, Daddy Bear took all the little bears outside. They played hide and seek, tag, and bear ball! Zachary Bear played too! Isaiah, Sarah, and Paisley had a wonderful time and hoped the night would not end.

Soon, Mommy Bear called everyone inside and said it was almost time for the three friend bears to go home. Daddy Bear had all the bears come together in the bear living room and told them a wonderful story. He told them how Jesus Christ was born of Mary and Joseph and that Jesus loved all the bears very much. It was the most wonderful story Sarah, Isaiah, and Paisley had ever heard.

Now it was time for the three bear friends to go home. They had plenty of time before dark but wanted to make sure they got home early enough to eat dinner with their families. Bear children are always hungry! Before they left, they gave big, warm bear hugs to their new friends. As they walked home, a light snow began to fall. They noticed again the beautiful Christmas lights and decorations as they made their way through town. The lights seemed to twinkle a little brighter, and the decorations glowed with a special warmth. And the three bear friends realized they had just been a part of the best Christmas ever.

On their way home, Isaiah Bear said to his friends, "You know, I don't need a new video game system. I will be happy with whatever Santa Bear brings me."

Paisley Bear said, "Yes, me too. And I will be thankful to spend time with my family this Christmas."

And Sarah Bear said, "Yes, I guess I'm thankful I have good legs and arms that I can play tag and hide-and-seek and bear ball with my cousins."

And as they went, not only were they thankful, but there was a new joy in their hearts that they tried to explain to each other, but no matter how they tried to say it, they were not able to put into words just how much joy they had. It was the best Christmas ever for Sarah, Isaiah, and Paisley—and it hadn't even come yet!

And at Hannah's house at bedtime, she and Kaitlyn Bear were in their pajamas and looking forward to the great day they would have in the morning. Daddy Bear and Mommy Bear came to tuck them in.

And Daddy Bear prayed over his precious girl bears and said, "Lord Jesus, thank you for the two best little bear girls I could

ever ask for. Please bless them for Christmas. And thank you for bringing Zachary home. Amen."

And as Daddy and Mommy Bear were leaving the room, Hannah Bear spoke up and said, "Mommy and Daddy—it's the best Christmas ever!"

About the Author

Matt Nichols is a husband, father, pastor, crusade speaker, and most importantly a lover of Jesus Christ. As a pastor, he loves to read a Christmas book to the children of his church on Christmas Eve. He found that although there are hundreds of books about Santa, elves, and reindeer, there are very few that speak about Christ. He wrote this book for the purpose of reading to the children in his congregation and is pleased to share it with you.

Pastor Matt regularly ministers to orphans in third-world nations and holds mass scale crusades. He pastors in a small town in Indiana. Although the town is just over two thousand residents, the church has well over one thousand members. Matt remembers in the year 2006 when he heard a still, small voice tell him that from this point (the rural church he pastored) he would touch the world. In addition to crusades and orphanages, Pastor Matt is featured on television programs around the world, telling people the good news of Jesus Christ. When Pastor Matt is not ministering, he enjoys spending time with his wife, Andrea, and their three children. He also enjoys boating, hiking, and traveling.

CPSIA information can be obtained
at www.ICGtesting.com
Printed in the USA
JSHW061825080922
30299JS00001B/5

9 781098 085551